This edition is printed and distributed by special arrangement
with the originators and publishers of
BEGINNER BOOKS, Random House, Inc., New York, by
E. M. HALE AND COMPANY

Ann Can Fly

by FRED PHLEGER

Illustrated by ROBERT LOPSHIRE

Beginner Books

A DIVISION OF RANDOM HOUSE, INC.

This is a big day for Ann.
Her father will take her to
camp in his new airplane.

Ann has never gone up in an
airplane. "Will it be fun?"
she asks. "Will I like it?"

Her father laughs.

"You will like it," he says.
"You will see."

At the airport, Ann can see
many, many kinds of airplanes.

Ann says, "Look at that little
plane, the one with the funny
things over the wheels."

"That is my plane," says Father.
"Those things are floats. The
floats will let us land on the water.
It is a good plane and it
will hold all your things."

"You were right," calls Ann.
"I can get all my things in.
Now can we go?"

"Not yet," Father says. "There are
a lot of things we have to do
first. Come, I will show you."

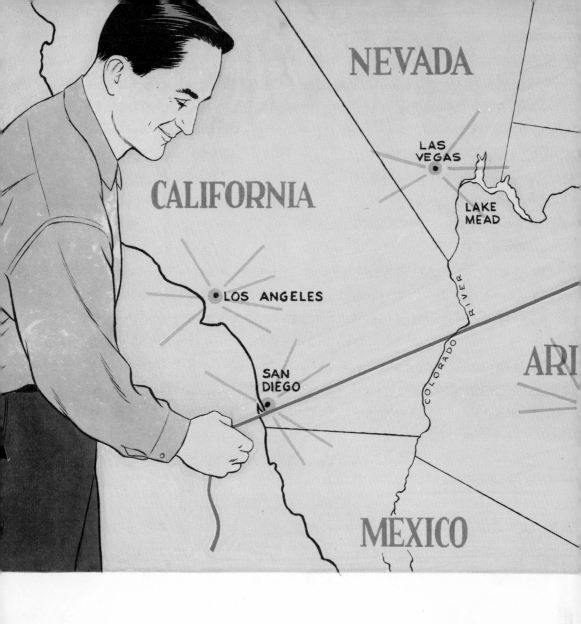

First, Father shows Ann
an air map.

He shows her the way they will
go to Camp Lake Wood.

"Now what do we do?" Ann asks.
Father says, "Now we have to
look at another map."

Ann can see that this new map is not like the other one.

This map shows where the wind is. It shows where the rain is.

The airport man says, "There is no wind and no rain where you want to go."

Father says, "Good. We can go back to the plane, now."

Father and Ann do not get into
the plane yet.

A man pumps gas into the plane.

Father looks the plane all over.

All the things are as they should be.

Now Father and Ann can get

into the plane.

Father makes the engine go.
He makes it go fast.

"We are all set now," he says.

"What do I do with my wheel?"
Ann asks.

Father laughs. "You do not do
a thing with it now," he says.
"You just put on your seat belt.
It will hold you down
if the plane bumps."

14

They ride up to the runway.

They are the first in line.

Now what?

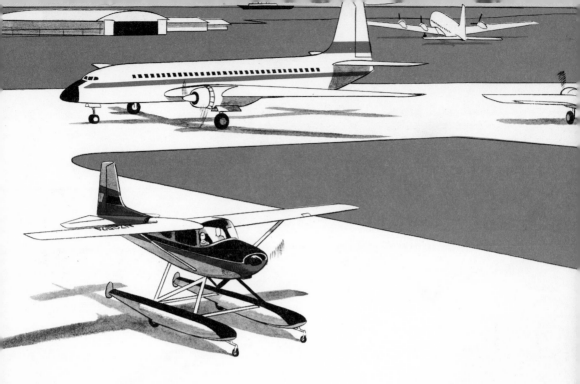

Ann hears her father call to
the airport tower.

"This is Airplane Seven Six
Nine Two. Can we go now?"

Ann hears the man in the tower
call back. "O.K., Airplane Seven
Six Nine Two. You can go."

"At last!" says Ann. "This is it!"

Away they go!

They go into the wind. Fast!

Father pulls back on his wheel.

This makes the wings of the plane

go up.

The wind gives the wings a big

push up. Now the plane is up!

The houses go by fast.

"My," says Ann, "this is something!

But I do like it."

They go up and up and up.
Now they are way up. They are
a long way from the airport.
There is another plane up here, too.

"Look," says Father, "we have to
get out of the way of that plane. It is
too near us."

"How?" asks Ann. "How do we get
out of its way?"

Father laughs.

"We will go to the right," he
says. "To do that I push my right
pedal down and I make my wheel go
to the right at the same time.
Your wheel does the same thing.
You could fly the plane
with your wheel, too."

"Oh," says Ann, "that
would be fun!"

"If you want to have more fun,
look down," says Father.

"We are just going over a new town.
See the houses down there?
Over on your right, you will soon
see a lake. It will be Lake Mead."

"Lake Mead!" says Ann. "I
see it. And I know all about
it. It is a man made lake."

"And we will land on it,"
says Father. "For we have to
get gas for the plane."

Father heads the plane
into the wind. The wind helps
to slow the plane down. Father
makes the engine go slow, too.

Down they go like a bird.

Down to land on the water!

They are down. Down on
Lake Mead! The two long floats
keep the plane on top of the water.
The floats splash water all over.
The plane is like a boat now.

Father heads the plane for
the gas pump.

Now they have the gas they want.

Away they go!

They go up! Up!

"How high we are!" says Ann.

"Do you want to know just how high we are?" asks Father. "See the little hand at 8. The big hand is at 0. That says we are now 8,000 feet high.

"Now, from way up here we will see the Grand Canyon. We will soon be near it."

The Grand Canyon is so big!
And it is so deep! There is water
down there in the canyon.

At one time that water was way up
on top of the land. Then the water
cut down and down into the
land. It took many years for it
to cut the Grand Canyon.

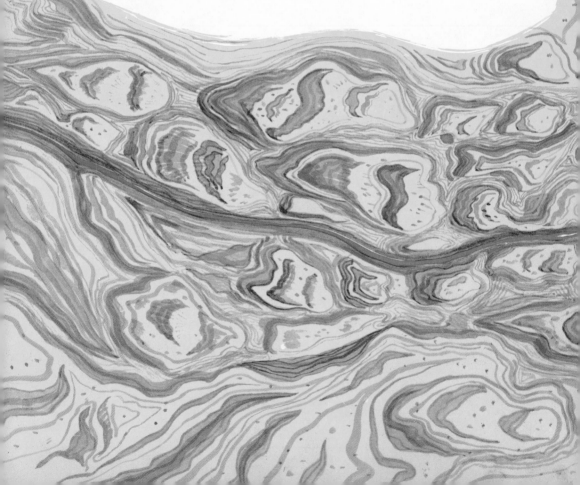

Ann and Father fly right over
the Grand Canyon. What fun!
They fly on and on.

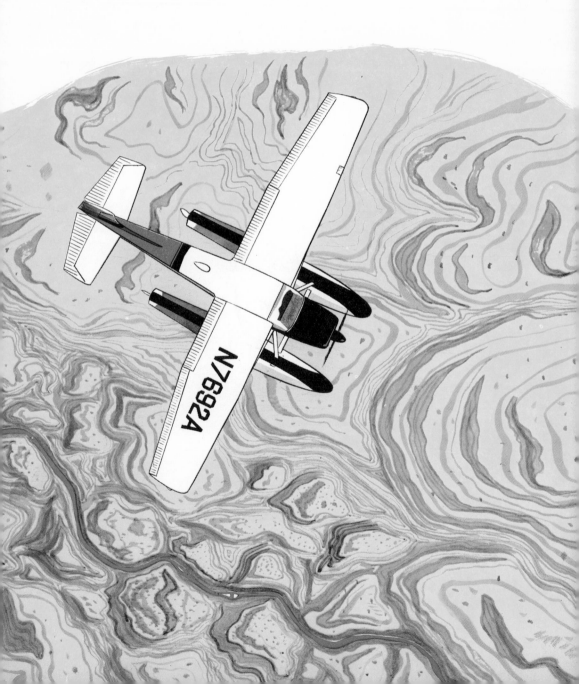

They are past the Grand
Canyon now. The sun is low.

"The sun is so red," says
Ann. "It is about to go down."

"We have to stop for the night,"
says Father. "We will land at
that little airport down there."

Father looks for the runway of
the airport.

And down they come.

There are many Indians here.

One of the Indians looks after

the plane.

"Come on, Ann," says Father.
"We will get something to eat.
Then we will go to bed, and
in the morning we will fly on
to Camp Lake Wood."

The next morning Ann and her
father are up with the sun.
The plane is all set to go.

Father calls to hear about the
wind and clouds. He hears there
are some clouds near Camp Lake Wood.
He hears they are not too big.

"Can we go?" says Ann.

"Yes," says Father. "A little
cloud will not hide the land. If
we can see the land, we can fly.
Let's go."

They can see all over.

There are no clouds at all.

There are no other planes.

Father looks over at Ann.

Ann has her hands on her wheel.

She wants to fly the plane.

"Go on," says Father, "you can
do it. I know you can. Take over!"

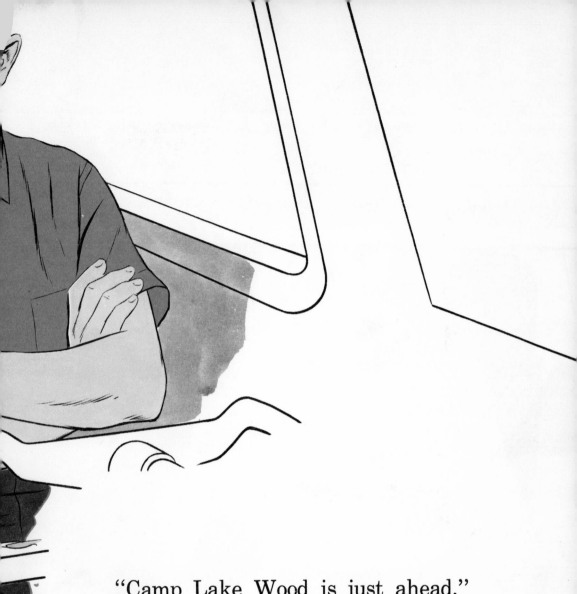

"Camp Lake Wood is just ahead,"
says Father.

"Hold on to the wheel. See,
Ann! You can fly the plane!"

"Look at me!" says Ann.

"Look at me fly!"

"I see you, Ann," says Father.
"But I see a cloud over there,
too. It looks like a bad one.
Where did that come from? I
will have to take the wheel now."

Now there is another cloud
right in the way.

They are black clouds. They are
rain clouds.

Father knows the two clouds
will soon be one cloud.

He does not like the look
of things up here. He takes
the plane down a little.

There are more clouds now.
They are all black. They have
come up fast!

Father says, "We must be near
your camp now. Look down for it."

Ann looks and looks. "I can't
see a thing," she says.

"Not one thing."

The clouds are all about them.

The wind bumps the plane.

The seat belts hold them down.

Now the rain comes. How it
rains! It rains and rains.

Father makes the plane go fast.
They fly on and on.

"Oh!" says Ann. "Look!
Look down there! There is a
little hole in a cloud! There
is the lake. Now look! I can
see the camp."

Father laughs.

"I can see it, too," he says.
"And am I happy to see it!"

Father heads the plane
right for the camp.

"Would you like to take the
wheel again?" asks Father.
"Would you like to fly the plane
over the camp?"

"Oh," says Ann. "Could I? The
girls will see me. They will know
I can fly."

Now Ann takes the wheel.

She takes the plane right over
the camp.

All the girls run out of the tents
and look up.

Ann calls down to the girls,
"Look! Just look at me fly!"

Her father laughs.

"They can not hear you, Ann," he says.

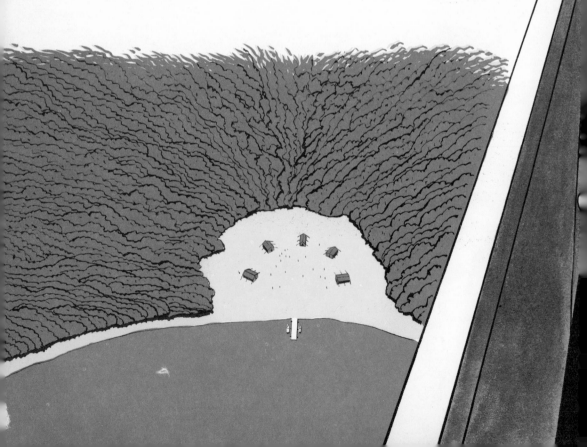

But that night at the camp fire,
the girls do hear Ann.

Ann tells them all about it.

"Some day you will fly," she
tells them. "You will like it.
You will see!"

When you see this smiling face of
the Cat in the Hat on a Beginner
Book, you can be sure that the book
can be read by beginning readers, and,
equally important, that they'll have fun
reading it. *Titles already published:* THE CAT
IN THE HAT, THE CAT IN THE HAT COMES
BACK, A FLY WENT BY, A BIG BALL OF
STRING, THE BIG JUMP and Other Stories,
SAM AND THE FIREFLY, YOU WILL GO
TO THE MOON, COWBOY ANDY,
ANN CAN FLY, THE WHALES GO BY,
STOP THAT BALL!, and BENNETT CERF'S
BOOK OF LAUGHS.